A Midsummer Night's Dream

About the Author

Beverley Birch grew up in Kenya and first came to England, where she now lives with her husband and two daughters, at the age of fifteen. After completing an MA in Economics and Sociology, Beverley became an editor at Penguin. Within a few weeks she was offered the chance to work on children's books and has been involved in children's publishing – as both editor and writer – ever since.

She has had over forty books published, from picture books and novels to science biographies and retellings of classic works. All her titles have received critical acclaim and her work has been translated into more than a dozen languages. Her latest novel for teenagers, *Rift*, was published in 2006.

Shakespeare's Tales

A Midsummer Night's Dream

Retold by Beverley Birch

Illustrated by Ted Dewan

WAYLAND

For my mother, with love

First published in *Shakespeare's Stories: Comedies* in 1988 by
Macdonald & Co (Publishers) Limited.
This edition first published in 2006 by
Wayland, an imprint of Hachette Children's Books

Cover and text design: Rosamund Saunders

Hachette Children's Books
338 Euston Road, London NW1 3BH

Printed and bound in the United Kingdom

ISBN-10: 0 7502 4963 3
ISBN-13: 978 0 7502 3963 8

The Cast

Duke Theseus – ruler of Athens
Hippolyta – his bride-to-be
Hermia
Hermia's Father
Lysander
Demetrius
Helena

THE WORKMEN
Peter Quince – the carpenter
Francis Flute – the bellows mender
Tom Snout – the tinker
Robin Starveling – the tailor
Snug – the joiner
Nick Bottom – the weaver

THE FAIRIES
Oberon – King of Fairies
Puck – a goblin, servant to Oberon
Titania – Queen of Fairies
Titania's Fairies

How slow the old moon waned! Four days until the bright new moon brought in the wedding day of great Duke Theseus.

Four days to watch the old moon lingering and dream of pleasures yet to come.

But with what triumph, pomp and celebration then would Theseus marry fair Hippolyta beneath the new moon's silver bow: though he had wooed and won her with the sword, now he would wed this Queen of Amazons with mirth and merriment and revelling through all of Athens.

There were others who watched the passage of the waning moon with anxious eyes. There was a girl of Athens named Hermia, whose father wanted her to wed

Demetrius, a rich and handsome youth most suitable as a husband. But Hermia did not love Demetrius. She loved Lysander, also rich and handsome, but to young Hermia's eyes so much finer than any other youth. Lysander had won her heart with poetry, by moonlight sung of love, showered her with tokens of his adoration, flowers, rings and locks of hair …

The father stormed against his daughter, who with her passionate tongue and stubborn disobedience refused Demetrius and declared her love for young Lysander.

The Father came in anger to Duke Theseus to demand the law against his rebellious child. Either she should marry the man he chose, or suffer the punishment decreed by law: death, or live out her days far from the company of men, locked in a nunnery.

Duke Theseus gave Hermia until the next new moon, his wedding day, to make her choice. On that day she must declare herself: either to marry Demetrius, as her father wished, or let the laws of Athens take their course.

The lovers would not yield. To be forced to choose their love through others' eyes! Rather, they would flee the laws of Athens, and marry without a father's or a duke's consent!

So they agreed, and in a wood outside the walls of Athens they arranged to meet, the following night, by moonlight ...

Demetrius, though fiercely scorned by Hermia, yet loved her passionately. But he was adored by another girl of Athens: Helena. Helena was Hermia's closest friend: since childhood they had played and shared together.

But now Helena, who loved Demetrius with all her body and soul, found that he merely spurned her passionate devotion, and emptied all his love on her *friend* Hermia! He had eyes only for Hermia's dark eyes, ears only for Hermia's rich voice. The more *Hermia* frowned on him, the more he loved her! The more *Hermia* showed her hate, the more he followed her.

While she, poor loving Helena, found only that the more she followed Demetrius, the more he hated her!

There was no sense or fairness in love's choices! Hermia was small and strong and dark with deep brown eyes and raven hair. Helena was tall and slim and fair with soft blue eyes. Many in Athens (as Helena told herself) considered her no less beautiful than Hermia, and before Demetrius had loved Hermia, he had poured out vows of love to *Helena.* When he saw Hermia these vows vanished like the dew before the rising sun, and left poor Helena trailing like a discarded pet.

But Helena would not give up, and she was desperate to find some favour, however small, in Demetrius' eyes. Learning from Hermia and Lysander of their plan to flee from Athens the following night, she resolved to tell Demetrius and lead him to where the lovers had arranged to meet, by moonlight, in the wood ...

These final days of the slow-waning moon had others in a flurry besides our tangled lovers. In a workman's house in Athens six men were gathered, six honest, earnest, hard-working men of that great city. There was Peter Quince the carpenter, Francis Flute the bellow's mender, Tom Snout the tinker, Robin Starveling the tailor, Snug the joiner; and last, but by no means least, Nick Bottom the weaver.

They planned a most important event for the celebrations of Duke Theseus' wedding day: a play, performed by them. And what a play their play would be! A story of tragic lovers such as there had never been in all the world: 'The most lamentable comedy and cruel death of Pyramus and Thisby': a very good piece of work, Bottom assured the assembled company, and helpfully urged Peter Quince to start by calling them, man by man, according to the parts that they would play.

Bottom the weaver was, in the eyes of all who knew him, a most worthy man, a man of many parts and many talents, a man who, amongst all the quantities of working men in Athens, *must* play Pyramus, the lover that kills himself for love …

Bottom was pleased with this. Why, it would call for a truly *dramatic* performance. It would draw tears in torrents from the audience, though he confessed he was more disposed to play a tyrant, for a tyrant could rant and rave. He leapt to his feet and bellowed lustily,

'The raging rocks
And shivering shocks
Shall break the locks
Of prison gates ... '

Now this was a part a man was made for! (A lover, he assured his friends, was more condoling ...)

Francis Flute was none too pleased to have to play the lady's part, for he had a beard coming.

'Let me play Thisby too!' cried Bottom with considerable relish. 'I'll speak in a monstrous little voice. "Thisne, Thisne,"' he demonstrated his tiny squeak with much flapping of 'elegant' lady's wrists, '"Pyramus my lover dear! Thy Thisby dear and lady dear!"'

The other parts were distributed with greater speed, for Bottom's imagination was not truly captured by mere fathers or mothers of the tragic lovers. But the *lion* – that was a part! If Snug the joiner was nervous of it, Bottom would do it! He would roar such a roar that the Duke would say 'Let him roar again!' Or, if that frightened the ladies in the audience, he could roar as gently as a dove, as sweetly as a nightingale …

It was, however, firmly established by good Peter Quince (who manfully wrestled control of the proceedings from the enthusiastic weaver), that Bottom must play *Pyramus.* This Pyramus was as sweet-faced a man as any you would see on a summer's day, a most gentleman-like man …

Bottom's thoughts had turned to the

question of the beard. What beard should Pyramus wear, he mused. Your straw-coloured beard? Your orange-tawny beard? Your purple-in-grain beard, your French crown-coloured beard, your perfect yellow?

With some effort, Quince managed to move on, for he had a final, most important communication to impart to his attentive company. *They must learn their lines.* By tomorrow night, they must all know them well. (Snug took this particularly seriously, for he was slow to learn, and was concerned to get the lion's roaring right.)

And so as not to have the whole of Athens know their plans, they would rehearse their play in secret. In the woods outside the town, they would all meet the following night, by moonlight …

The wood lay silver-tipped beneath the moon, each blade of grass, each leaf and branch soft-stroked with liquid pearl. It was a place of whisperings and shimmerings, of watching eyes green-glowing like fire beneath the giant trees.

It was a place of magic. It was bewitched by more than the moon's caress across the darkened glades.

It was the realm of Oberon, King of Fairies, and of Titania, his silver queen. No human eye could see them, no human ear could hear them, but they were there, woven in the rugged oaks that bowed across the moon-washed world, threaded in the murmuring earth, floating on the lilt of brooks and the sweet wind that sighed across the leaves.

And tonight this wood was haunted by more than the joyous revels of fairies, elves and sprites, for it trembled beneath the King of Fairies' anger at the Fairy Queen.

Titania had, as her attendant, a lovely human boy taken from an Indian king. How she loved and cherished this changeling child! But Oberon was jealous: he desired the boy to be a knight of his train, to wander the wild forests with *him* …

And now these proud and passionate monarchs never met on hill or dale, in forest grove or meadow green, but that their bitter quarrel soured the air, poisoned the winds and turned the earth to misery. Because of them, dark fogs and bitter frosts had wrapped the warmth of spring in winter's shroud; unripe corn lay rotting in the field, and swollen rivers drowned the meadows and the villages.

And still Oberon demanded the changeling boy to be his henchman, and still Titania withheld him, crowned him with flowers and made him all her joy. Now, though they flew from the far corners of the earth to bring their blessings to Duke Theseus' wedding day, still their old quarrel flared anew …

'Ill met by moonlight, proud Titania!' Oberon hailed her, and the great oaks trembled with the anger of this powerful lord of the dark place, while all his tiny elves drew close behind their master.

Titania's fairies peeped from the silver glow that wrapped their dancing queen.

'What, jealous Oberon,' Titania cried.

'Fairies, skip away. I have foresworn his bed and company!'

He stepped towards her, fierce. 'Why should Titania cross her Oberon?' he challenged her again. 'I do but beg a little changeling boy to be my henchman!'

'The fairy land buys not the child from me!' Titania sang and danced away from the dark thunder of her husband's eyes. 'His mother was of my following; for her sake I do rear up her boy, and for her sake I will not part with him!' And away she flew, her lilting voice echoing in Oberon's ears with mocking taunt.

He brooded on her disobedience, and the brooding filled his soul. *She* would not leave this forest glade till he had tormented her for his injury! He called his attendant to him, a

shrewd, prick-eared goblin known as Puck, much given to pranks and roguish tricks. To him, the King of Fairies gave his secret orders. There was a tiny purple flower called 'love-in-idleness' that grew far off in the western lands …

'Fetch me that flower,' he breathed. 'The juice of it laid on sleeping eyelids will make man or woman madly love the next live creature that it sees. I'll watch Titania when she is asleep, and drop the liquid on her eyes. The next thing that she, waking, looks upon, be it lion, bear, wolf or bull, meddling monkey or busy ape, she shall pursue it with the soul of love … Fetch me this herb, and be here again before the whale can swim a league!'

'I'll put a girdle round about the

earth in forty minutes!' chanted Puck, and disappeared.

And Oberon brooded on his plan; while Titania languished in bewitchment, he could spirit away the changeling boy …

But Oberon's mischievous thoughts were suddenly and violently disturbed: a raucous clamour tore the air, the sound of quarrelling human voices, the crash of *human* feet! Being invisible, he hovered close to hear these rash intruders entering his domain.

It was Demetrius, blundering through the undergrowth in search of Hermia. But he was followed, as he always was, by love-lorn Helena. In vain he tried to shake her off. He yelled. He frowned. He shouted. But she was there, her love-sick gaze still drinking in each word and look of his as though they were the nectar of the gods themselves.

'I cannot love you!' he shouted, for perhaps the hundredth time.

'And even for that I do love you more,' she sobbed. 'I am your slave, the more you beat me, I will fawn on you. Use me but as your slave, spurn me, strike me, neglect me, only give me leave to follow you … '

'I am sick when I must look at you,' the desperate youth declared.

'And I am sick when I look not at you,' the wretched girl replied.

And Oberon, festering with his own lovers' quarrel, was touched by the unhappy Helena's plight. He vowed a second vow that night: before Helena could leave his forest realm, Demetrius would seek her love and she would fly from him.

Now Puck alighted at his side and held aloft the magic flower. Oberon seized it. It caught a glancing moonbeam and gleamed purple in the cloaking dark. He stroked it, murmuring, and the wind took up his words and sowed them in the trees ... 'I know a bank where the wild thyme blows, where oxlips and the nodding violet grows. There sleeps Titania sometime of the night, lulled in these flowers ... '

And then, with sudden anger he cried out, 'With the juice of this I'll streak her eyes and make her full of hateful fantasies!'

His gaze now fell on eager Puck, ever ready to follow his master's wish. 'Take some of it,' he ordered him. 'Seek through this grove. A sweet Athenian lady is in love with a disdainful youth. Anoint his eyes with this,

and do it when the next thing that he spies will be the lady. You shall know the man by the Athenian clothes that he has on.'

Titania slept, while fairy sentinels drooped drowsily and did not see the Fairy King creep close to her, nor see him squeeze the magic juice across her eyes, nor hear his murmured words …

'What thou seest when thou dost wake,
Do it for thy true love take
Love and languish for his sake
Be it lynx, or cat, or bear
Leopard, or boar with bristled hair.
Wake when some vile thing is near.'

Below the sleeping Fairy Queen two other lovers came into the glade: Lysander and the beautiful Hermia, now much begrimed and stuck with twigs and leaves. They had lost their way in this strange wood, and now they were foot-sore and desperately craved sleep. In the morning, fresh, they could resume their flight from Athens.

'Good night, sweet friend,' Hermia whispered to Lysander. 'May your love never alter until your sweet life ends.'

'Amen to that fair prayer,' the loving youth replied. 'And let my life end when I end loyalty ... '

They settled down together in that dappled glade (but not too close together, till the bonds of marriage were tied up). And so it came about that wandering Puck, seeking Demetrius and Helena, *now* came upon this sleeping couple. He noted the youth's Athenian clothes and the young woman lying some little way away: at once he assumed *this* was the young woman so churlishly rejected by the youth that Oberon had seen. Swiftly he poured the magic juice across Lysander's eyes, and sped back to his master's side.

For a moment the glade was quiet. And then the crashing in the undergrowth began again; into the glade stumbled frantic Demetrius, still running from a more than frantic Helena. With a final furious shout at her, he plunged on into the wood, so that she stood now, quite alone amid the looming trees.

It seemed now that no plea, no prayer could work its charm on scornful Demetrius, and Helena despaired. She ached with tiredness. She slipped and slithered in the dark, seeking a place where she could sink to rest. As she did, she stumbled across sleeping Lysander. Afraid he might be hurt, she shook the youth, and Lysander, waking with his eyes streaked with the magic juice, saw Helena and fell instantly, passionately, in love. All thoughts of Hermia took flight (how tedious seemed the hours spent with her). Who could still love a raven such as Hermia beside this glowing, dove-like Helena?

Helena stared at Lysander now in greater misery than ever before. What had she done to draw this mockery from others? It was not enough for Demetrius to spurn her, but Lysander must add to her injuries by playing his own games with her! It was too much for any girl to bear! And Helena rushed frantically from the glade, Lysander in hot pursuit of this, his most passionate new love.

Hermia, quite ignorant of the magic changes in her lover's heart, slept on, until a dream of crawling serpents woke her violently. Alone? Lysander gone? No answering shout to greet her? Only a thousand night creatures' glinting eyes!

In terror she ran off, shrieking for Lysander ...

To this same wood, at midnight, came the six working men of Athens, prepared to do their play exactly as they would before Duke Theseus. They tramped into the moonlit glade and looked around (a little apprehensively, if each were to admit it to the other).

'Here's a marvellous convenient place for our rehearsal,' Quince declared. 'This green

plot shall be our stage, this hawthorn bush our dressing room.'

Bottom had been thinking very seriously. 'There are things in this comedy of Pyramus and Thisby that will never please,' he told them soberly. 'First, Pyramus must draw a sword to kill himself, which the ladies of the audience cannot abide … '

Snout, Starveling and Flute all nodded: the killing must, undoubtedly, be quite left out.

Bottom had pondered his way towards a better answer. They must have an introduction to their play – a *prologue* (he said the word proudly to give it full effect) – and this prologue would say that they would do no harm with their swords, and that Pyramus was not really killed, and (to reassure them thoroughly) Pyramus was not *really* Pyramus, but Bottom the weaver.

An excellent solution!

In the trees about their makeshift stage there lurked an unseen watcher who observed their earnest efforts with amusement.

'What hempen homespuns have we swaggering here, so near the cradle of the Fairy Queen?' bright Puck enquired, for his mischievous nose had sniffed out the flavour of some teasing frolic for his entertainment.

Unknowing of their hidden audience, the players now began. Bottom, as Pyramus, was first. 'Thisby, the flowers of odious savours sweet,' he declared, most eloquently.

'*Odours, odours,*' interrupted Quince.

'Odours savours sweet,' said Bottom

obligingly. 'But hark! A voice!' and right on cue, he disappeared into the hawthorn bush.

There was a silence. All eyes turned expectantly to Francis Flute. It dawned on him, though slowly, that they were all waiting for *him*.

'Must I speak now?' he asked, nervously.

'Aye,' said Quince, most patiently. 'Pyramus goes but to see a noise, and will come again.'

Promptly (before he lost his nerve), Flute spewed out all his lines at once in a great flood, and left nothing more to speak in the rest of the play.

Quince sighed deeply; 'You must not speak that yet,' he said, in a tone of utmost world-weariness. 'Pyramus, enter!' he called. 'Your cue is past … '

But hovering Puck had suddenly devised

the merriest prank of all. Following Bottom into the hawthorn bush, he had swiftly touched the weaver's ears, which, in no more than the blinking of a goblin's eye became long, furry, flapping ears; his nose, which grew into a long, bony nose; his eyes, which became the large, dark, somewhat bewildered eyes of an enormous, hairy ass!

Bottom, unaware of this miraculous transformation, reappeared at Quince's call with gusto.

'If I were fair, Thisby,' he announced with passion, 'I were only yours!'

His companions stared. They blinked. They backed away. They trembled. And then, with one panic-stricken howl, they fled.

Somewhat bewildered, Bottom watched his friends run out, run back again, stare, shriek, point fingers, gibber, peer at him from behind the trees and disappear again ...

Why did they run? Some joke of theirs, to come and gawp and run again!

'Bless you, bless you, Bottom, bless you!' Quince whispered in awe. 'You are transformed!'

This was unmistakeably a ruse to frighten him, Bottom decided. If only they could! He looked about him at the giant trees, standing sentinel about the grove. They loomed, they leaned ...

He shook himself. 'I will not stir from this place,' he declared. 'Do what they can, I will not stir. I will walk up and down here. And I will sing. And they shall hear I am not afraid!' this last he yelled defiantly across the silent grove. And he burst forth,

'The ousel cock so black of hue

With orange-tawny bill

The throstle ... '

Cushioned on her bed of flowers, Titania stirred, then stretched and woke. And as she did, her eyes, charmed by the flower-juice, fell on this valiant figure with the head of a great ass and body of a sturdy, somewhat portly, man; and instantly this queen of gossamer light fell wildly, insanely, in love with him.

'What angel wakes me from my flowery bed?' she breathed.

The object of her adoration stamped on across the grove, thump, thump, thump, thump; then back again, clump, clump, clump, clump, and then he bellowed even louder to warn the looming shades of night *they* could not threaten him.

'The finch, the sparrow and the lark
The plain-song cuckoo grey … ' he carolled.

And then he stopped, for now he saw the silver vision decked in moonbeams float across the grove, and heard her, with a voice like tinsel bells of flowers, speak to him …

'I pray you, gentle mortal, sing again. Mine ear is much enchanted by thy note. So is mine eye enthralled by thy shape … and I am moved to say that I do love thee.'

Bottom was not a man ever at a loss for long. He prided himself on this. Silver visions who sang of love in moonlit woods notwithstanding, he *would* maintain his true sense of proportion at all times …

'I love you,' the lady sang.

'I think, mistress,' he said, sensibly, 'you should have little reason for that; and yet, to say the truth, reason and love keep little company together nowadays … '

'Thou art as wise as thou art beautiful,' the wondrous lady murmured.

'Not so, neither,' he assured her, 'but if I had wit enough to get out of this wood … '

'Thou shalt not go,' her music voice sang on. 'Thou shalt remain here, for I do *love* thee … Therefore go with me,' the lady whispered in his ear (the great, tall ass's ear that twitched a little for her lips were tickling him). And away she drew him, and wove her spells about him: she would give him fairies to attend on him and grant his every wish; he could sleep on heady flowers while their perfumes wafted him to sleep; he could feed on apricots and dewberries, on purple grapes

and mulberries, on honeybags stolen from the bumble bees; her fairies would fan moonbeams from his sleeping eyes with wings of butterflies.

Bottom, refusing to be bewildered by the orderly procession of tiny fairies before his eyes, was always a polite man. Each one, in turn, he addressed with courteous concentration, made sure he asked each name, and shook each hand (though this was somewhat difficult with hands that seemed to slip like moonlight through his fingers).

'Tie up my love's tongue,' the silver lady whispered. 'Bring him silently … '

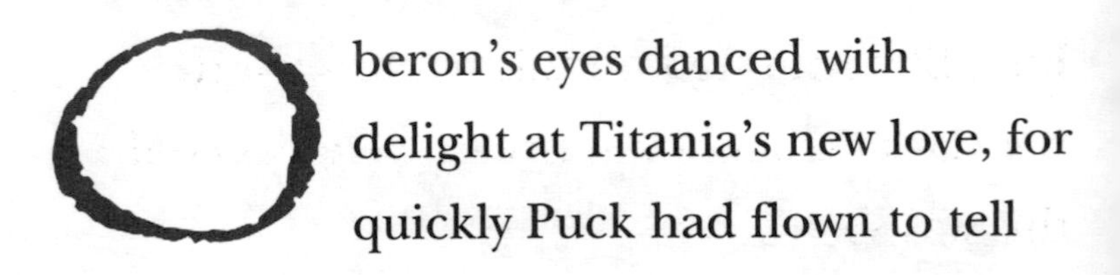

Oberon's eyes danced with delight at Titania's new love, for quickly Puck had flown to tell his master, and to amuse him, too, with tales of how he led the other workmen a merry caper from the woods, scrambling and slithering as they were through briars and thorns to escape that haunted place.

And here, to add to Oberon's delight, came the Athenians. Swiftly the dark king and his impish henchman vanished, to watch the spectacle unseen.

Young Hermia came flying in, pursued by passionate Demetrius. She, though much irritated by the persistence of this unwanted youth, was more concerned at the disappearance of her love, Lysander. A thought struck her. Demetrius had killed him! She rounded on this hapless youth, her dark eyes flashing instant vengeance if this was so.

Demetrius gave up. He was growing a little weary of this chase, for it gave so few rewards. He was exhausted by these endless hours chasing through this endless wood. Foot-weary, and in great ill-humour, he left Hermia to run on, and lay down on the ground, to sleep.

Oberon rounded on the meddling Puck. Demetrius still loved Hermia! He had not shifted his affections to fair Helena!

No, Puck admitted (much amused by this spectacle of squabbling humans), this was not the Athenian he had charmed ...

'About the wood go swifter than the wind,' Oberon gave orders, angrily. 'Find Helena of Athens. Lead her here, by magic.' And while Puck flew off to do his bidding, Oberon alighted on the ground near Demetrius, and swift as wind he charmed Demetrius' eyes in time for Helena's appearance.

Puck was much enjoying himself, for mischief was the food of life to him. In a twinkling of an eye he was back, to sing,

'Captain of our fairy band,
Helena is here at hand.
And the youth, mistook by me …
Lord, what fools these mortals be!'

Two youths, who both loved Hermia, to be translated into two who both loved Helena! No greater fun could Puck imagine!

Helena's bewilderment at Lysander's loud vows of undying love had turned to fierce indignation. She was desperate to get away from him, to escape this cruel mockery. Stumbling in the moonlight across the forest glade, Lysander close behind, she fell across

Demetrius. He woke, and saw the woman he had scorned so bitterly now coloured by the love-flower's enchanted mists.

'Helen, goddess, nymph, perfect, divine!' he cried. 'To what, my love, shall I compare your eyes? Crystal is muddy! Oh, let me kiss this princess of pure white, this seal of bliss!'

Helena fell back in disbelief. They were hell bent to use her for their merriment! It was not enough that Demetrius should hate her, as he had made plain, now he joined with Lysander to taunt her pitilessly!

'You would not use a gentle lady so,' she begged, 'to vow and swear your love when I am sure you hate me in your hearts. You are both rivals and love Hermia. Now both rivals you mock Helena!'

To simplify this tangled knot, Lysander

grandly donated the absent Hermia (whom he no longer loved) to Demetrius.

Demetrius, who had loved Hermia wildly until a few moments ago, now scorned the gift. He loved *Helena*, adored *Helena*, would worship *Helena* for ever more.

Into this hornets' nest came Hermia, still fretting at Lysander's disappearance from her side, yet with his vows of loyalty to her still echoing in her ears. She saw him now and rushed to his side. 'Why did you leave me so unkindly?'

But why should he stay, she heard Lysander's cold and unfamiliar voice. Love drew him on!

She stopped. She looked from him to Helena, from Helena to Demetrius. She heard again these words her ears could not believe. Her own true love's lips now shouting at her to go and leave him, declaring the *hate* he felt for her!

Helena, watching this extraordinary scene, saw it all clearly now. It was a plot between all three of them! *Hermia* was at the root of it. This *friend*, with whom she had shared all vows of childhood, was locked in conspiracy with these cruel men, to scorn and bait her!

'Oh, is it all forgotten? All school-days' friendship, childhood innocence?' she sobbed.

Hermia stopped the stream of words. 'I do not scorn you, it seems you scorn me!' In disbelief she heard Lysander's voice. 'My love, my life, my soul, fair Helena! Helen I love you, by my life I do.'

And then Demetrius, bristling against his

rival, 'I say I love you more than he can do!'

'If you say so,' Lysander shouted, 'withdraw and prove it!'

'Quick, come!' Demetrius yelled, and drew his sword.

Now Hermia understood. She rounded on her friend. 'You juggler! You canker-blossom! You thief of love! What, have you come by night and stolen my love's heart from him?'

'You counterfeit! You puppet!' shrieked Helena back, convinced that this was all still part of their dreadful plot.

'Puppet!' bellowed Hermia. 'Now I see she compares our heights! With her personage, her *tall* personage, her height, no less, she has won him!' She danced in rage before her willowy friend. 'And are you grown so high in his esteem because *I* am so dwarfish and so short? How short am I, you painted maypole? Speak! How short am I? I am not so short that my nails can't reach your eyes!'

'Let her not hurt me,' shrieked Helena. 'Let her not strike me. When she is angry she is keen and shrewd. She was a vixen when she went to school, and though she is little, she is fierce!'

'Little again! Nothing but little!' screamed Hermia, and flew at Helena. Lysander thrust shrinking Helena protectively behind him.

Demetrius shouted belligerently, 'Do not take Helena's part!' and once again they were circling each other, like spitting cats …

And then (so as not to use swords before the ladies) they went off to find a place to fight for Helena's love, still glaring wildly at each other.

Oberon looked at Puck, and his look was like the thunder before it erupts from a glowering sky.

'This is thy negligence!'

'Believe me, King of Shadows,' Puck sang out, 'I mistook ... did you not tell me I should know the man by the Athenian garments he had on? I have anointed an Athenian's eyes!' (But, mistake or not, what sport to see these mortals jangling!'

'These mortals seek a place to fight,' bellowed Oberon. 'Hurry and overcast the night with fog, black, black fog to lead these rivals far astray that they may never meet each other! Then crush this herb into Lysander's eye,' and his look allowed no meddling pranks or disobedience this time.

This miserable confusion must be set to

rights and Lysander's vision turned from Helena to Hermia again. But haste, haste, for the night was paling fast, and all must be accomplished before the break of dawn ...

The impish Puck did as his master ordered, gleefully. He danced and floated in the mists, calling now in Demetrius' voice to wandering Lysander, now in Lysander's voice to stumbling Demetrius; now in a bush, a tree, across the brook, now far behind, now far in front, now up, now down, egging each on until their legs grew weary, their flesh stung with pricks and scratches and each separately, ignorant of how close the other stumbled in the mists, lay down to sleep until daybreak could release them from this misery.

And then the ladies came: first, Helena, smeared with mud, her dress in shreds and longing now for nothing but the sunlight's warmth so that she could escape this hideous place and friends who detested her enough to play these cruel jokes. She lay down to sleep.

'Yet but three?' grinned hovering Puck.

'Come one more;

Two of both kinds

Makes up four.

Here she comes, cursed and sad!'

Hermia could go no further. Though she still longed to find Lysander and stop the fight, she was so soaked with dew, so torn with briars that she was almost crawling …

And she too lay down to sleep.

Now they were ready for Puck's magic: each close together, though they did not know it, each near their chosen love.

He dropped the herb on to Lysander's sleeping eyes.

'On the ground

Sleep sound

I'll apply

To your eye,

Gentle lover, remedy.

When you wake

Take true delight

In the sight

Of your former lady's eye.'

Invisible to the lovers' eyes, a stranger company than they could ever imagine now came among them.

'Come sit upon this flowery bed while I caress your cheeks and stick musk-roses in your sleek, smooth head, and kiss your fair, large ears, my gentle joy,' Titania's cooing voice enticed the weaver on.

Bottom was much enjoying this unlooked for holiday from the workaday existence of a sober Athens weaver.

'Where's Peaseblossom?' he asked. 'Scratch my head, good Peaseblossom. Where's Monsieur Cobweb? Good monsieur, fetch me a red-hipped bumble bee on the top of a thistle; and good monsieur, bring me the honeybag; and have a care that the honeybag does not break. I would be loath to have you overflown with a honeybag, signor.' He settled luxuriously into the bower of flowers. 'Where's Monsieur Mustardseed?'

'What's your will?' a tiny voice came to his languid ears.

'Nothing, good monsieur,' said Bottom generously, 'but to help Monsieur

Peaseblossom scratch. I must go to the barber's, monsieur,' he assured him, seriously, 'for I think I am marvellously hairy about the face ... '

He yawned. And if the wondrous fairy lady would cease her stroking and allow him, he was now ready to sleep ...

'Sleep,' her voice was in the wind, and in the leaves, 'and I will wind thee in my arms. So does the woodbine entwine the sweet honeysuckle ... Oh, how I love thee! How I do dote on thee!'

And Titania, too, slept, wound round her love. She did not know this passion was the work of jealous Oberon, nor that he had already seized the changeling boy while she lay wrapped in adoration of Bottom the weaver's ass-headed charms.

Their purpose won, two moon-dappled shadows came among the lovers to undo the charms. Oberon bent low across his queen and spoke the charmed words that would undo the spell that bound her. He called her, gently, 'Now, my Titania, wake, my sweet queen.'

She woke, and saw him bending over her, and looked about her, startled. 'My Oberon! What visions I have seen! I thought I loved an ass.'

'There lies thy love,' murmured Oberon, and as she backed in horror from poor Bottom, blissfully ass-headed on the ground, the King of Fairies took her hand.

'Come my queen, take hands with me, and rock the ground whereon these sleepers be!' And so these monarchs of the moonlit night joined hands, new-tied in bonds of love, and dancing in a magic circle blessed the sleepy lovers on the ground.

Tomorrow night their fairy dance would bless the triumph of Duke Theseus' wedding day, but as the morning lark raised his shrill cry, they vanished, to follow the shades of night to other lands ...

With the morning lark came others to that forest glade. Duke Theseus and his bride-to-be Hippolyta were revelling in their long-awaited wedding day. Before daybreak they had risen to follow the hounds and hunting horns into the woods, and they stood now, listening to their swelling music across the hills and valleys. They paused in the sunlit glade to catch the scent of morning in the flowers, and stumbled, much to their surprise, on the four lovers, fast asleep and lying close together on the ground.

'Go bid the huntsman wake them with their horns,' Duke Theseus commanded.

To the triumphant bay of unleashed hounds and bray of horns across the western valley, the startled lovers woke. They stared at the wondering audience, looked at each other, tried to stammer out an explanation of their presence there, but found they could not really find one …

'I came with Hermia,' Lysander remembered, suddenly, and turned with love towards her. All memories of adoration felt for Helena had flown with waking sight of Hermia …

And by some power which he could not understand, Demetrius now found himself in love with Helena and not with Hermia!

And so they stood there, once four lovers running in a ring about a moonlit wood, now two loving pairs: Lysander and Hermia, Demetrius and Helena, who still could not believe her ears were not playing tricks on her when she heard Demetrius' declaration of his love for her before the *Duke!* 'All the faith, the virtue of my heart, the object and the pleasure of my eye is only Helena,' he said!

Duke Theseus saw at once how perfectly the tangled knot had been untied, and how the thorny problems set by Hermia's father were now resolved. It was a splendid outcome for his own, most glorious, wedding day, and he was in no mood to let a father's anger at the thwarting of his wishes mar its pleasures or the happiness of these young people, so in love.

Swiftly he decided. He would overrule the father if he was still disposed to press an unwanted marriage on his reluctant daughter. 'In the temple, by and by with us, these couples shall eternally be knit in marriage,' he said. 'Away with us to Athens! Three and three we'll hold a feast in great solemnity!'

And with his bride-to-be upon his arm, he swept from the sunlit glade, leaving the bewildered lovers quite alone. They looked at each other curiously. Each wondered if the others had heard and seen what they *thought* they had seen in this strange and misty night just passed ...

'These things seem small and indistinguishable, like far-off mountains turned into clouds,' murmured Demetrius, wonderingly.

'I seem to see these things with parted eye, when everything seems double,' said Hermia.

'And I have found Demetrius, like a jewel, my own,' sang Helena, who could think of nothing else.

'Are you sure that we are awake?' Demetrius still wondered. 'It seems to me that yet we sleep, we dream.'

And yet Duke Theseus *had* been there, *had* bid them follow him to Athens. On that they all agreed.

They linked arms, chattering suddenly like magpies about the night's events, and followed the Duke's party from that forest glade.

The glade was silent now, warm-lit by morning sun. Gone were the flitting shadows of the night who flew on moonbeams from tree to tree. Gone were the lovers, babbling of their dream.

The sun blazed down and wrapped the sleeping Bottom in its golden blanket. He dreamed on, and on. He mumbled in his sleep. He murmured softly, laughed, stretched, and laughed again.

And then slowly, he began to wake, luxuriously. 'When my cue comes, call me, and I will answer,' he murmured. 'My next is, "Most fair Pyramus ..."' He stretched again. Then he sat up. He looked about him. No one there? He called, 'Peter Quince! Flute! Snout! God's my life, stolen away and left me asleep!'

Then he remembered: a woman of silver light who stroked him, loved him, sang to him, and he wafting on sweet beds of flowers, her king! A life of song and drowsy luxury, of idleness beyond his dreams … He almost swooned again with memories.

'I have had a most rare vision,' he assured himself. 'I have had a dream, past the wit of man to say what dream it was. I thought I was … ' he shook the thought away. 'There is no man can tell what,' he announced conclusively to the slumbering wood. 'I thought I had … ' he began again.

And again he shook his head. 'The eye of man has not heard, the ear of man has not seen, man's hand is not able to taste, his tongue to imagine or his heart to report, what my dream was,' he addressed the brooding oaks … and for a moment he was wandering in his dream again, lost in its ecstasies … 'I will get Peter Quince to write a ballad of this dream,' he announced with more certainty, 'and it shall be called Bottom's dream, because it has no bottom … '

At Quince's house Bottom's friends despaired. A play without Nick Bottom? A play without their Pyramus? Bottom was the Pyramus to beat all Pyramuses, the tragic lover to beat all lovers. They trembled to think what might have happened to him. Had he been carried off by spirits, transformed (before their eyes) into a monster? Or was it all a nightmare they would wake from, happily?

'Where are these lads?' the booming tones

of Bottom sang along the street. 'Where are these good fellows?'

They gaped, searched wildly for the ass's head they had last seen on him. Seeing nothing but their good friend's jovial face, they promptly leapt with joy, clapped him on the back, danced several jigs around him, and all at once there was a flurry of excited preparations.

Costumes ready? Strings to their beards? 'Let Thisby have clean clothes,' urged Bottom enthusiastically. 'And let him that plays the lion not cut his nails, for they shall hang out like the lion's claws. And, most dear actors,' he called them back, 'eat no onions nor garlic, for we are to utter sweet breath; and I do not doubt but to hear them say, it is a sweet comedy. No more words! Away! Go! Away!'

The lovers came now, wed, to while away the hours before their wedding night with jovial entertainment: and a jovial entertainment it certainly promised to be: 'A tedious brief scene of young Pyramus and his love Thisby; very tragical mirth,' the company of actors announced themselves.

The young couples settled comfortably, prepared to be much amused by the efforts of these earnest working men who had so worked to bring this 'tragic' tale to Theseus' celebration.

They little knew what scenes of mirthful tragedy *they* had played before another audience in a silver wood not so very far away ...

Wall came first. With trembling wide-eyed

face above the chink made by his parted fingers, he explained this was the hole through which the tragic lovers Pyramus and Thisby would whisper secretly.

'Would you desire a wall to speak better?' Duke Theseus enquired of his fellow watchers approvingly.

They hushed as Pyramus crept in, soft-footed, and with much staring gloomily about him to ensure there was no doubt he came in *dangerous* secrecy.

'Oh grim-looked night! Oh night with hue so black!

Oh night which ever is when day is not!' he wailed.

'Oh wall oh sweet lovely wall!

Show me thy chink to blink through with mine eyes!'

Dutifully Wall held up two fingers.

'Thanks, courteous Wall,' said Bottom with tears of heartfelt gratitude in his eyes. He peered through the chink.

'But what see I? No Thisby do I see!' he rolled his eyes and clutched his heart.

'Oh wicked Wall!' he beat the Wall's sturdy breast (Wall staggered a little beneath the impassioned onslaught but withstood it sturdily). 'Cursed be thy stones for thus deceiving me.'

'I think the Wall being able to talk, should curse again,' Theseus whispered rather loudly to Hippolyta.

'No! In truth sir he should not!' Bottom was most perturbed to find there was some confusion on this point. '"Deceiving me" is Thisby's cue,' he explained patiently to the confused Duke. 'She is to enter now and I am to spy her through the wall. You shall see … here she comes!'

Unfortunately for Bottom, Francis Flute was having a little trouble with his yellow wig. It would fly off whenever he tried to move. He clasped it firmly to his head and lolloped on, kicking the folds of his dress valiantly aside (though he had quite forgotten to change his boots).

Suddenly, and alarmingly, he was facing this distinguished audience. He peered owlishly at them, trembled with the seriousness of his forthcoming task, and squeaked determinedly.

'Oh Wall, my cherry lips have often kissed thy stones.'

'I see a voice,' gasped Pyramus, relieved

to see his partner finally appear beyond the looming shape of Wall. 'Now will I to the chink!'

At this most poetic exclamation, the audience, who had been merely tittering, now dissolved in uncontrollable laughter.

'Oh kiss me through the hole of this vile wall,' shrieked Pyramus, now much enjoying himself and gathering momentum since the audience seemed to be having so much fun ...

'I kiss the wall's hole, not your lips at all,' piped Thisby.

'Wilt thou at Ninny's tomb meet me straight away?' yelled Pyramus.

'I come without delay,' lisped Thisby from beneath the crooked wig, for it had now slid disconcertingly across one eye.

And out they marched, arm in arm, forgetting they were still two lovers separated by a wall …

Wall, left alone before a giggling audience, shuffled from foot to foot, summoned what remaining courage he had and belted out his lines at top speed.

'Thus have I, Wall, my part discharged, and being done, thus Wall away doth go!' and without further ado, he fled.

The audience waited expectantly. Lion came on (Snug's face peering reassuringly from beneath the shaggy head), and spoke a pretty speech to explain he was really Snug the joiner, and no fierce lion.

'A very gentle beast,' Duke Theseus approved, 'and of a good conscience.'

Now it was Moonshine's turn. Much

encouraged by the loud noises emitting from the audience, he waved his lantern enthusiastically and yelled, 'This lantern presents the horned moon. Myself the man in the moon do seem to be!'

On cue, Thisby clumped in, saw the lion, who duly roared a mighty roar. Thisby ran off shrieking, then ran on again, propelled by Peter Quince, to throw her cloak down on the ground. Lion seized the cloak, and with several lusty roars, tore it to shreds. Pyramus rushed on, saw the mangled cloak, assumed his lover Thisby dead, whipped out his sword, plunged it in his own breast, and fell moaning and grimacing with pain.

'Now am I dead
Now am I fled
My soul is in the sky

Tongue, lose thy light

Moon take thy flight!'

Though this last was not in the script as he remembered it, Moonshine took Pyramus at his word, and galloped off.

Thisby, wig restored, rushed on.

'What, dead my dove?

Oh Pyramus, arise, speak, speak.

Quite dumb?

These lily lips, this cherry nose,

These yellow cowslip cheeks,' she intoned, warming greatly to the scene now that the play was nearly done.

And so the tragedy of Pyramus and Thisby galloped to its close, affording its audience no less transport of mirth and sheer delight than the antics of that same audience had once offered the sprightly Puck in that far-off, dream-washed, moonlit world outside the walls of Athens.

The palace was now quiet. The newly-weds had all retired to bed, wrapped in the magic of their love. And now a different magic came to touch Duke Theseus and his bride Hippolyta.

It was at first only a shimmering, and then a gentle whispering, a silver breeze that stirred across the halls, the kissing touch of shadows dancing with tinsel sounds across the moonbeams in the rooms …

They came, the King of Fairies and his queen, with all their train of fairies, elves and sprites led by bright Puck, to bring their blessing to this house and all who slept in it …

Or was it no more than a moonlit dream from an enchanted midsummer night?